T0142683

Spiritual SPORTS

Five Life Lessons for Players and Parents with Zeus the Zebra

· ·

KATHY FAIN COUGHLIN

Balboa Press books may be ordered through booksellers or by contacting:

Balboa Press
A Division of Hay House
1663 Liberty Drive
Bloomington, IN 47403
www.balboapress.com
1 (877) 407-4847

ISBN: 978-1-9822-4764-5 (sc)
ISBN: 978-1-9822-4763-8 (e)

Library of Congress Control Number: 2020908806

Print information available on the last page.

Balboa Press rev. date: 02/17/2021

BALBOA®PRESS

A DIVISION OF HAY HOUSE

I dedicate this book to my Dad

My Hero

My Champion

My Role Model

The one who taught me to measure myself
from "My Shoulders to the Sky"

Spiritual Sports

Five Life Lessons for Players and Parents with Zeus the Zebra

Spiritual Sports

It's me, Zeus, the Zebra. Even though I am not very tall,

I LOVE basketball!

I make up for my height by playing with heart.

That's what sets me apart.

I have a coach that is wise and smart.

He tells me to always play with my heart.

Since my coach has played on several courts,

he took me aside and asked if I played Spiritual Sports?

"What's that?" I asked. He said, "don't be scared to play, don't fear it."

"Play for the LOVE of the game, play from your spirit!"

Most of the time, kids play to be #1.

That turns out not to be any fun.

That's when kids start to quit.

It's a sign they don't play from their spirit.

Play for those life lessons and learn the valuable things.

Don't count wins or championship rings.

Even the pros don't win every contest.

Then, there's no pressure to be the best.

You can't force a player to have an inner drive.

If you keep working hard, you will arrive.

When I play from my spirit, I remember to pass to my team.

I love to see them smile and their confidence beam.

I feel the love for just being out there.

I show the team how much I really care.

When I play for the love of the game, it lasts forever!

It teaches me to love the journey and love the endeavor.

Whether or not I am always #1,

I know that I played for the love of the game and I had fun!

Class on the Court

It's me, Zeus, the Zebra. Even though I am not very tall,

I LOVE basketball!

I make up for my height by playing with heart.

That's what sets me apart.

I work hard every day.

I put the time in, so I can play.

I have a great coach, who works with me on every skill.

He tells me to be persistent and have a strong will.

My coach tells me that I can either make an improvement or an excuse.

I am strong! I am Zeus!

I am the smallest zebra on the court.

I am full of confidence, I must report.

I don't let size stop me.

I can be anything that I want to be.

I measure myself from my shoulders to the sky!

If I put my mind to it, I can fly!

I pride myself on being a good teammate.

With hard work and hustle, I know my fate.

My story is about how to act on the court.

No matter the circumstance, be a good sport!

Control what you can and that's not a lot.

You can't control if you make every shot.

What you can control is how you act.

That's not a myth. That's a fact.

Problems occur and you are not alone.

Don't complain and don't moan.

Refs will miss calls, it's part of the game.

If you argue, you are the one who will look lame.

Nobody likes a bad sport.

Have Class on the Court!

Win or lose, a competitor will have a smile on their face.

Play with class, play with grace.

I hope you have liked my sportsmanship way.

Take it with you when you play.

The Power of Gum

It's me, Zeus the Zebra. Even though I am not very tall,

I LOVE basketball!

I make up for my height by playing with heart.

That's what sets me apart.

Parents, fans...You don't need to suffer through this sporting event.

Just count the blessings you have been sent.

Don't look for what's wrong, catch something going right.

It may not be easy, it may take all of your might.

If you don't like what you see,

Here's a tip to set you free!

You don't have to bite your tongue at all.

Chew GUM when your kids play basketball!

Keep your mouth busy, so not to criticize or attack.

Be supportive, so that your kids know that "you got their back."

Don't add to their pressures or their fears.

Sit back quietly full of cheers.

Oh, and don't dis the coaches plan.

Be grateful for the time that he puts in and be an encouraging fan.

Let's face it, they are probably not going to the NBA.

So, teach them by example how to overcome tough times when they come their way.

Don't blame coaches, refs, or circumstance.

Kid's don't need to hear any more negative rants.

Instill a vison: There's nothing they can't overcome.

Blow a few bubbles with your gum.

Relax, it may take a bubble or two.

Before you speak, try something new.

How you handle things shows what you are made of.

All you need to do is send out love.

Your kids will notice and be so proud.

Of how their parents act in the crowd.

Don't stress out over this game's outcome.

Just sit back and chew your GUM!

How May I Assist?

It's me, Zeus, the Zebra. Even though I am not very tall,

I LOVE basketball!

I make up for my height by playing with heart.

That's what sets me apart.

As you were probably guessin'...

Here I am with another life lesson.

Here's a twist...

Ask the team and coach, "How may I Assist?"

Instead of saying, "Look at me, I am in my prime."

What about me and my playing time?

Be willing to give up your starting spot.

Or is it better defense that you need to plot?

Does the team need you to cheer from the side?

Or step up as a leader and guide?

Instead of thinking about yourself and it's all about me...

Open your mind to the power of WE.

Instead of focusing on your shot and your playing time.

Throw passes to your teammate on a dime.

It's okay to set some goals.

Teammates are best when they play their roles.

Don't just play for the glory.

Let go of your own personal story.

Don't play for the credit that you are due.

Open your mind to a brand new view.

Take my advice,

be unselfish and don't think twice.

Ask your coach if you can try what most players can't do.

Put the team before YOU!

Give high fives and in the team huddle, raise your fist.

Ask your team, "How may I Assist?"

A Champion's Mind

It's me, Zeus, the Zebra. Even though I am not very tall,

I LOVE basketball!

I make up for my height by playing with heart.

That's what sets me apart.

I am going to tell you about my championship game.

And how my life was never the same.

The game started. The ball was tipped.

We were confident, we didn't think that we would be whipped.

I promise you that we paid our dues.

We were sure that the other team was going to lose.

We started the game with a confident swagger.

An attitude of class, not that of a bragger.

To our surprise, we were wrong!

The other team was just too strong.

We found ourselves down 20 points at the half.

We didn't doubt, or cry, or laugh.

We told our coach, "Don't worry and don't count us out."

We said, "We got this" with a mighty shout!

We won't give up, we're still in.

We will play to win.

We came up with a plan. Let's stop their top guy.

Coach said, "Together we can do it, let's try."

Our team captain said, "Coach, can we play a box and one?"

We did just that and the other team was done.

Their best player said, "Just try to stop my outside shot and I will post you up and take you down low."

Our team pulled together and said, "I don't think so!"

Not only did our team defense stop their top guy.

We pledged to each other to...never give up and to never say die!

We worked too hard to go out that way.

We lived to fight and play another day.

We all would hustle and dive on the floor.

We were too focused to even hear the crowd roar.

We decided to do whatever it takes.

Our defense caused fast breaks.

Our team was in the zone.

All the other team could do is moan.

We took our team to a higher place.

Everyone on the team put on their "game face."

Our teamwork was a beauty to behold.

Our team refused to fold.

What caused this game turnaround?

A champion's mind! We were the ones crowned!

This was a game we would remember for the rest of our lives.

We were so proud, all that we could do is give each other high-fives!

Knowing your own greatness is in a champion's mind.

Remember that if you are ever in a bind.

Bring a higher energy to your team.

It is only then that you will realize your dream.

Know that you can always come from behind.

Because victory is born first in your mind!

About the Author

Kathy Fain Coughlin is a skills trainer and the owner of Fain Fundamentals basketball training.

She is also a youth basketball league director.

As a player, she is known for having the State of Michigan assist record for the most assists in a season and two games in which she accomplished a quadruple double for points, assists, steals and rebounds.

As a coach, her varsity team won the Michigan National Guard Sportsmanship Award in 2010.

She enjoys spending time with her husband and two kids.

Printed in the United States
By Bookmasters